Madison Morris Is NOT a Mouse!

CLASS CRITTERS

Book 3

Madison Morris Is NOT a Mouse!

By Kathryn Holmes
Illustrated by Ariel Landy

AMULET BOOKS • NEW YORK

Cataloging-in-Publication Data has been applied for and may be obtained from the Library of Congress.

ISBN 978-1-4197-5569-9

Text © 2022 Kathryn Holmes
Illustrations © 2022 Ariel Landy
Book design by Jade Rector and Brann Garvey

Printed and bound in U.S.A.
10 9 8 7 6 5 4 3 2 1

Amulet Books® is a registered trademark of Harry N. Abrams, Inc.

ABRAMS The Art of Books
195 Broadway, New York, NY 10007
abramsbooks.com

For McKay

Doing Big Things

"You're late," Madison Morris's great-aunt grumbled as Madison's mama helped her climb into the car.

She said the same thing every Thursday. Madison and her mama were never late.

Still, Madison knew better than to argue. "Good morning, Great-Aunt Joelle!" she chirped.

As Mama walked around to the driver's side, Great-Aunt Joelle twisted in the passenger seat, giving Madison a critical look. "That top isn't very flattering."

Madison was wearing a neon-pink T-shirt with a yellow sun on the front. It was the most cheerful thing in her dresser. She loved it.

"Those colors," her great-aunt went on, shuddering. "So . . . bright."

This was how Great-Aunt Joelle was. The first time she'd seen Madison's new cornrows, she'd said, "I don't like those braids. Your hair looks better straightened." When Madison had explained that the cornrows were easier to manage *and* better for her hair—never mind how cool they made her feel—Great-Aunt Joelle had simply grumbled, "Hmph."

Mama got in and started the car. "All set?"

"Yes, ma'am," Madison said.

Great-Aunt Joelle grunted.

It had been Madison's idea to pick up her great-aunt on Thursday mornings. Great-Aunt Joelle's apartment building was on the way to Madison's school. The school was near the YMCA. On Thursdays, the YMCA offered free exercise classes for senior citizens. Exercise was supposed to make people happy.

Of all the grown-ups Madison knew, Great-Aunt Joelle was the one most in need of a happiness boost. It hadn't worked yet . . . but it was only a matter of time.

"Madison," Mama said, "did you tell your great-aunt about your project?"

"Well?" Great-Aunt Joelle snapped, as if she'd been waiting and waiting.

"We're doing a unit on activism," Madison said.

"Activism." Great-Aunt Joelle muttered the

word like it was something gross, like *cock-roaches* or *snot* or *gorgonzola cheese.*

"We've been learning about kids who have done stuff to change the world," Madison went on, "and now we're talking about what we could do as a class to help our community."

Mrs. Norrell had asked her students to each come up with one idea for a class project. Today, they were going to take turns sharing those ideas. Then, they were going to vote on which project to do.

Madison was desperate to have the winning idea. So she hadn't come up with just *one* potential project. She'd filled page after page after page with them.

"Do you want to hear some of my ideas?" she asked, grabbing her notebook.

Great-Aunt Joelle made a sound that could be either a yes or a no.

Madison chose to hear a yes. She started at the top. "We could clean up around the creek—"

4

Great-Aunt Joelle interrupted her: "It'll be trashed again before you know it."

Hm. Madison took her pencil and drew a line through *Creek Cleanup.*

"We could trade library books with another school," she said next.

Great-Aunt Joelle scoffed. "There's no way they'd return your books in one piece."

Oh. Madison didn't like to see books get damaged. She crossed out *Book Swap*.

"What about gathering cans for the food pantry?" she tried.

"A few cans aren't going to solve world hunger."

Huh. So much for *Food Drive*.

Mama sighed. "Aunt Joelle . . ."

"What? The girl needs to be realistic about what she can and can't do."

"I can do a whole lot," Madison said.

Great-Aunt Joelle laughed. "You're a child."

"Kids can do big things," Madison insisted. "Kids are already doing big things! Marley Dias was only eleven when she started collecting books about Black girls to donate to schools and libraries. And Mari Copeny was even younger than that when she wrote to the president about her city not having clean water—"

"Children," Great-Aunt Joelle pronounced as they entered the school parking lot, "should be seen and not heard."

Mama sighed again. "Madison, honey," she said, pulling up to the curb, "have a wonderful day. And keep dreaming big, okay?" She reached back for a hand-squeeze.

"Always." Madison squeezed with all her might.

The last thing she heard as she shut the car door was her great-aunt's skeptical snort.

Leadership Material

Madison stood in the doorway to her class-room, smiling with anticipation.

She loved being helpful more than she loved just about anything. More than homemade cherry cobbler, which was her favorite dessert. More than llamas, which were her favorite animal. More than sunflowers, which were her favorite plant. Helping people was better than homemade cherry cobbler and llamas and sunflowers combined.

Almost exactly as much as she loved being helpful, Madison loved being in charge. Or at least . . . she loved the *idea* of being in charge. No one had actually put Madison in charge of anything important. Not yet. That was why today mattered so much.

Her dad was the boss at his office. He'd told Madison how being a boss worked. You had to come up with a plan. That was called strategizing. You had to give people jobs to do. That was called delegating. You had to make sure the jobs were done the right way. That was called supervising.

When her dad's employees were ready to take on more responsibility, he liked to say they were "leadership material." Madison knew *she* was leadership material. At the Morris family reunion over the summer, Madison had kept an eye on the little kids while they splashed in the sprinklers *and* she'd made sure all the elders had fresh, cold lemonade and iced tea without having to leave their comfy lawn chairs. (Doing two things at once, her dad said, was called multitasking.)

Keeping toddlers and old folks happy at the same time hadn't been easy, but Madison had managed it. Now it was time to tackle an even bigger challenge.

Every leader had to start somewhere. For Madison, today was the day.

"Madison!" Lydia Lee, Madison's best friend since preschool, waved from the back row. She was standing with their new friend, Tally Tuttle. Tally was cradling a rolled-up poster in her arms like it was a baby.

"What's that?" Madison asked Tally as she reached them.

"It's my community project," Tally said. "I want to build a habitat for the wild turtles that live in the creek behind the school. I drew a diagram."

"Wow," Madison said. "That's a good idea. Can I see your poster?"

"She said it's a secret," Lydia informed Madison.

Tally blushed. "It's not that I don't *want* to show you," she said. "I'm just nervous."

"You'll do great," Madison assured Tally. "What about you, Lydia?"

"I want our class to paint a mural in Founder's Park. My mom helped me research the permits we'd need," Lydia said.

"That's a nice idea, too," Madison told her best friend. Lydia was an artist, so whatever she designed was sure to be beautiful.

Mrs. Norrell clapped her hands. "Okay, class, find your seats!"

Tally sat right away. Madison and Lydia hurried two rows up to their side-by-side desks.

While Mrs. Norrell made morning announcements, Madison opened her notebook in her lap. She wanted her friends to do well, but . . . she really wanted to have the winning idea herself. So, she needed to present something that was even better than a turtle habitat or a mural.

As Madison traced her finger down her list, a strange thing happened. The ideas she'd been so proud of last night didn't seem quite right anymore. It wasn't just the ones she'd crossed out in the car. Suddenly, none of them were good enough.

She heard Great-Aunt Joelle's voice in her head:

The girl needs to be realistic about what she can and can't do.

Oh, no.

What if Madison wasn't leadership material after all?

Seen and Not Heard

Madison tried not to panic. Maybe it would help to hear more of her classmates' ideas. Then, she could figure out which one of hers had the best chance of getting picked.

As soon as morning announcements were over, Mrs. Norrell said, "It's project time! Who wants to kick us off?" The teacher scanned the room.

Madison slumped in her chair, hoping Mrs. Norrell wouldn't call on her.

Mrs. Norrell called on her.

"Madison! You're always eager to volunteer. Want to get us started?"

"No, thank you," Madison said quietly, glancing down at her list.

"Oh!" Mrs. Norrell sounded surprised. "Are you sure? We'd all love to hear from you."

Inside Madison's mind, Great-Aunt Joelle's disapproving voice said, *Children should be seen and not heard.*

"Maybe later," Madison said.

"All right. We'll come back to you," Mrs. Norrell said kindly. "Padma, would you like to tell us your idea?"

Padma began talking enthusiastically about raising money to build a playground at a tiny park near her house. "It doesn't even have a swing set!" she said, wide-eyed, like she could hardly believe her own words. "Every park should have a swing set!"

Madison agreed. Playgrounds were awesome—especially ones with swing sets.

Why didn't you *think of building a new playground?* her imaginary great-aunt asked.

Nate proposed connecting local kids who were into science with children their age in other places who also loved doing experiments. They could run the same tests and compare results. "I call it"—he did a drumroll on his desk—"Science Pals! Like pen pals, but . . . with science."

Madison could imagine other science-y kids like Nate being really into Science Pals.

Nothing you thought up comes close to that, the Great-Aunt Joelle in her head taunted.

Lydia talked about her mural. Tally talked about her turtle habitat. David wanted the class to meet one Saturday a month to walk shelter dogs. Gavin proposed putting on a comedy show at the retirement home. Even surly Victoria had a nice idea: Mrs. Norrell's second graders could visit a preschool class for one-on-one reading time.

Madison wanted to be supportive . . . but all she could think about was why everyone else's ideas were better than her own.

Great-Aunt Joelle wasn't with her at school. Great-Aunt Joelle was at water aerobics— hopefully becoming less of a grouch with each set of flutter kicks. But the old woman's voice kept getting louder and louder, until Madison couldn't hear anything else.

Your ideas are not special. You don't deserve to win the vote.

You are not leadership material. At this rate, you never will be.

Mrs. Norrell is disappointed in you.

You should be disappointed in yourself.

Before long, Madison had scribbled through every idea in her note-book. Mrs. Norrell would call on her again soon, and she had nothing to say. She felt as small as a mouse.

A cool breeze danced across her warm brown skin, giving her goose bumps.

Somewhere in the distance, a balloon popped.

There was a strange smell—citrus air freshener mixed with stinky skunk-spray.

"Ew." Madison wrinkled her nose. The motion made her whiskers twitch.

Hold on.

Madison didn't have whiskers.

Just like she didn't have grayish-brown fur or pinkish paws or a tail or . . . she swiveled the rounded ears that sat on the top of her head. Nope, she didn't have those, either.

She'd felt small a minute ago, but now, she actually *was* small. Which was all wrong.

Madison Morris was NOT a mouse!

A Squeak of Triumph

Her heart . . . it was beating so fast inside her tiny body. The sensation reminded her of her last birthday party, when she'd had too much confetti cake and grape juice and had gotten what her nana referred to as the sugar-shivers. She tried taking a deep breath to calm herself down. It didn't help.

Maybe she'd fallen asleep. Maybe this was a dream.

She'd been in her chair, at her desk—

Well, technically she was *still* in her chair, at her desk. She was just crouched on all fours,

instead of seated on her bottom. She shifted her weight onto her back legs, using her tail for balance as she lifted the front half of her body. Sitting upright, she felt more like herself. Thank goodness for her tail, propping her up.

Except . . . she shouldn't have a tail.

She wasn't a mouse.

She lost her balance and toppled back onto all fours.

At the front of the room, Mrs. Norrell cleared her throat. "Um . . . where was I?" She rubbed at her forehead. "Oh, yes. Now that we've heard from everyone—"

"Wait!" Madison squeaked. "What about me?"

"I'll make a ballot," Mrs. Norrell went on as if Madison hadn't spoken. "We'll have a vote in between lunch and recess. I can't wait to see which project you all pick!"

Madison began to pace on her chair. She couldn't win the vote and get put in charge of their class project if she hadn't even shared any ideas. What was she going to do?

"While I type up our ballot, you can have independent reading time," Mrs. Norrell said.

"No!" Madison screeched as loud as she possibly could.

From the seat directly in front of her, Aaron asked, "Did you hear something?"

"Yeah, maybe," Lydia said from Madison's right.

"Lydia! Down here!" Madison shouted.

"It's like . . . a tiny whistle," Lydia said, confused. "Where's it coming from?"

And then Victoria screamed.

Mrs. Norrell put her hand to her heart. "Victoria! What on earth—"

"A mouse!" Victoria pointed a trembling finger at Madison. "In Madison's chair!"

"David, did you do this?" Aaron asked. David had brought his puppy to school for show-and-tell a couple weeks ago, so it was a reasonable question.

"I *wish* it was me!" David answered, already moving to get a closer look.

"I want to hold it!" Farrah squealed, jumping to her feet.

"No, me!" Chase hurdled over the back of his chair to beat Farrah to Madison's desk. He scooped Madison up and cupped her between his palms.

"Let me go!" Madison squeaked.

He didn't.

In Chase's hands, Madison felt hot and penned in, like she was inside a fleecy sleeping bag that was zipped all the way around. Then everything got shaky as Chase began to move . . . toward Victoria, Madison guessed, because the other girl yelped, "Keep it away!"

"Keep what away?" Chase teased. "This cute . . . widdle . . . mouse?"

Their voices were muffled, but Madison's saucer-shaped ears were powerful. They were definitely stronger than her eyes, which couldn't really make out anything other than a thin seam of light between two of Chase's fingers. She turned toward that light, getting an idea.

"Victoria," Chase said, "are you telling me you don't like . . . *this*?"

The gap between his fingers got wider. Madison poked her nose and whiskers through it.

Victoria shrieked.

"Chase! Bring the mouse to me!" Mrs. Norrell shouted.

Madison wiggled in Chase's hands. She brushed her tail along his palms.

Chase laughed. "That tickles!"

Madison wriggled and shimmied and shook until Chase finally let her go. With a squeak of triumph, she launched herself out of her classmate's hands and into the open air.

Strengths and Weaknesses

Victoria let out more piercing shrieks. The sound made Madison's newly sensitive ears ring. It hurt way worse than when she'd had her cornrows put in, the stylist pulling the braids tight to her tender scalp. This was like having needles poked directly into her brain.

But Madison had bigger things to worry about than an aching head. Beneath her, the floor was getting closer and closer. Were mice like cats? Would she land on her feet?

Or would she simply . . . splat?

She did neither. Instead, she hit Tally's backpack with a soft thump. Nestled in the mint-green fabric, she took a moment to rest. Her heart was beating even faster than it had when she'd first transformed. Her whole body trembled and her breath was going *in-out-in-out-in-out-in-out*.

"Everyone, in your seats." Mrs. Norrell prowled between the rows of desks, holding a shoebox. "I'll catch it."

"Why do you need to catch it?" Farrah asked.

"If it's a classroom pet, it needs to go back to its cage. If it's not a pet . . ."

Madison wasn't a pet. She also wasn't a wild animal. Either way, she didn't think she wanted to get caught.

She spotted a small water bottle pocket on Tally's backpack. It was the perfect size for a mouse hideaway. She darted inside, did a U-turn at the bottom, and poked her head back out.

Okay. She was safe. She could think.

When her dad had talked to her about strategizing, he'd said listing your strengths and weaknesses could help you come up with a plan. He'd been discussing being a boss and leading a team, but maybe the same advice would work now. What were Madison's strengths and weaknesses, as a mouse?

Size: teeny-tiny. Eyesight: not great. Hearing: really good. Smell . . . she sniffed the air. The classroom seemed to have a lot more scents than usual, so she put her nose into the "strengths" category.

And then there were her whiskers. They were telling her all sorts of things. Like which way the air was flowing in the room. And not just from the air-conditioning. When people moved, they pushed the air around them. There were . . . vibrations.

Madison sensed vibrations above her. She looked up. Tally was staring down at her.

"Eek!" Madison dove into the pocket.

Her whiskers noted a whoosh in the air, as if Tally were bending over. "I don't know if you're Madison," Tally murmured, sounding like her face was right next to the backpack, "but if you are, there's someone you should talk to."

What? How could Tally possibly know Madison was a mouse?

There was another whoosh—a moving-away one, like Tally was straightening in her seat.

"Mrs. Norrell?" Tally said.

"Yes?" the teacher replied.

"Madison forgot something for her activism project."

"Oh." Mrs. Norrell's voice got cloudy. "Madison . . . yes."

"She's in the office, calling her mom," Tally said.

"Of course," the teacher said. "I remember."

What Tally was saying didn't make sense. In order for Madison to go to the office by herself, Mrs. Norrell would had to have given her the hall pass. The hall pass was still hanging on its hook by the classroom door.

Why would Tally make up such a story? Why would Mrs. Norrell believe it?

The air vibrated again. There was a gentle nudge against Madison's hiding spot. "Come on out," Tally whispered. "You can trust me."

Madison didn't have a clue what was happening to her, or why, but she *did* trust Tally.

Slowly, she emerged from the pocket and climbed out onto her friend's waiting fingers. Tally stood, holding Madison close to her body. She walked across the room toward the shelf that held the books for independent reading time. As she passed Bagel the guinea pig's cage, she slipped Madison between the bars.

"You'll be safe here," Tally whispered. "Good luck."

A Tiny, Happy Pop-Pop

"**Hello there!**"

Startled, Madison dashed into the hidey-house in the center of Bagel's cage.

Outside the shelter, there was a chuckle. "Sorry about that. Didn't mean to scare you."

Madison peered out from the shadows. "Bagel?" she asked. "Is that you?"

"Sure is!" The class pet wore a kind smile on his furry face. "Welcome, welcome." Bagel's voice was old and wise and warm. He sounded like a tiny, happy pop-pop. Like Madison's own pop-pop, in fact, but if he were only about four inches tall.

"Hi." Madison crawled out into the open. She looked around, wanting to make a good impression despite the strange circumstances. "I, um . . . I like your cage."

"Thanks! Me too!" Bagel tilted his head to peer at her. "But I bet you have some other things you'd rather talk about. Right, Madison?"

Madison gasped. "How do you know who I am?" If Tally knew, and Bagel knew . . . "Does my whole class know?"

"They do not. When this happens, things get a little . . . foggy for everyone else."

"When what happens?"

"Just a second, I'll explain everything." Bagel dug a little pit in his wood shavings. "First, hide down here."

"Okay." Madison burrowed into the hole.

Bagel brushed a few wood chips over her, camouflaging her grayish-brown fur. Then he came around to sit by her face. "Cozy?" he asked.

"Very," she said, and meant it. The wood chips smelled nice. Their weight on top of her tiny body made her feel a little less fidgety. She had an urge to gnaw on something, so she grabbed a large wood chip and bit down. Ahh. That hit the spot.

Bagel folded his front paws together. "Here's the deal," he said. "The kids in Mrs. Norrell's class sometimes turn into animals."

Madison almost dropped her wood chip. "What?! That's impossible." She didn't mean it in the way Great-Aunt Joelle liked to say things were impossible—meaning, difficult and complicated and therefore not worth doing. Madison meant it literally. "People don't just turn into animals."

"Then what happened to you?" Bagel asked.

After a beat, Madison said, "Fine. I turned into a mouse. Can you change me back?"

"Unfortunately, I can't. The magic doesn't come from me. It's just . . ." The guinea pig waved one paw in the air, looking out into the classroom. "Here." His gaze snapped back to Madison. "But only for Mrs. Norrell's students."

"If you can't fix me, what do I do?" Madison had gnawed her wood chip down to dust, so she grabbed another one. "I'm not stuck like this, am I?"

"Definitely not." Bagel puffed out his chest. "At least, not with me here to guide you!"

"Guide me how?"

"To turn back into your human self, you'll need to return to the exact spot where you changed. In your case . . ." Bagel pointed toward Madison's empty chair.

"I can do that," Madison said, feeling more confident. "Then what?"

"You have to think about *why* you turned into an animal. Everyone has a reason. Once you realize why—" Bagel stopped, squinting at her. "You know, I usually do this talk later in the day. Are you sure you're done being a mouse? You haven't been one for very long."

"Oh, I'm done," Madison said firmly.

"But . . . what did you learn?"

"I learned," Madison said, "that I am *not* a mouse!"

There was a moment of silence.

"Well," Bagel said doubtfully, "if you're certain."

"One hundred percent."

Inside Madison's head, Great-Aunt Joelle chuckled as though her great-niece had said something that was both funny and foolish. Madison tried to ignore how bad that chuckle made her feel.

"Thanks for your help," she said to the guinea pig. "I have to go change back now."

Before Bagel could say another word, Madison zipped between the bars of the cage.

All Pretzeled Up

Madison's classmates were reading. Mrs. Norrell was at her desk, typing on her computer. The coast was clear. Madison scampered along the shelf, looking for a way down—or at least a soft place to land. She ran past something, stopped, and doubled back.

There was a piece of cardboard taped to the back of the shelf. It looked like . . . a slide.

She peered into the darkness. She couldn't see very far. She sniffed the cardboard. She ran her whiskers over it, trying to sense how sturdy it was. Could she ride it down to the floor?

She brushed her whiskers over the cardboard again, mapping out the slide's dimensions. It was definitely wide enough for her tiny mouse body. It seemed thick enough to hold her weight. Even though she'd never had whiskers before today, she knew she could trust what they were telling her.

She jumped and slid.

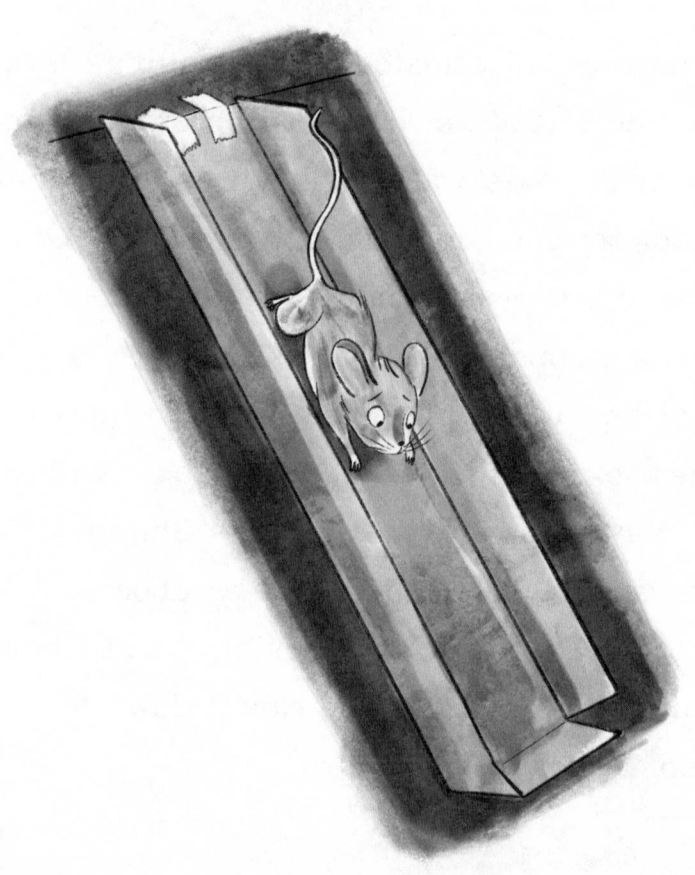

She hit the ground running. She dashed along the back wall behind Owen, Farrah, Padma, Victoria, Tally, and Nate. She turned right and raced under the bookshelves on that side of the room. Even though her eyesight wasn't great, her whiskers helped her dodge the dusty broken pencils, bent paper clips, and other debris in her path.

Her desk was in the second row from the front. She was almost there.

Her backpack was slouched against the legs of her chair. She wondered if she could jump from the bag to the seat. How high could mice jump, anyway?

She crossed the two floor tiles between the bookshelf and her desk and climbed onto her bag, her sharp claws digging into the fabric. She tried not to slow down too much as she prepared to launch.

She pushed off. She was airborne!

She . . . wasn't going to make it.

Her front claws hit the edge of the seat. She scrabbled and scratched, but the surface was too smooth. Unlike the backpack, there was nothing to hold on to.

She landed in a disappointed heap.

The Great-Aunt Joelle in her head cackled with vicious glee.

Madison tried to shake off the near miss. She could try again. Except . . . when she'd landed, she'd squished the backpack down an inch. If she hadn't been able to reach her seat before, how could she possibly get there now?

Maybe it would be okay to be beside her chair instead. Or even under it. Madison imagined herself reappearing—*poof!*—beneath her seat, arms and legs all pretzeled up to fit. It was a funny mental picture, but this was no time for giggling.

This was a time for action.

I am Madison Morris, she thought. *What I learned today is, I am not a mouse.*

Nothing happened.

She scrunched her eyes closed. She concentrated so hard, her whiskers trembled. She thought, as loudly as she possibly could: *I am a human being! I am NOT a mouse!*

When she opened her eyes again, she was still a mouse.

Now she felt all pretzeled up on the inside.

Great-Aunt Joelle was still laughing.

"Okay, class," Mrs. Norrell said. "I've typed up our ballots. I'll print copies during lunch. Because we have so many wonderful ideas to consider, each of you can choose your top three. We'll narrow it down from there."

Madison moaned. If she couldn't get an idea on that ballot—and not just any idea, the *very best* idea—how would she ever become the leader she was meant to be?

Tally came to her rescue yet again. "What

about Madison?" she asked. "She's still, um, in the office. Can we wait for her?"

"Oh." Mrs. Norrell nodded slowly. "I suppose I can add her idea to the list later, before we vote."

Madison let out a long breath. She still had a chance.

An Epic Climb

According to Bagel, if Madison wanted to stop being a mouse, she had to get up onto her chair. That clearly wasn't going to be as easy as she'd thought. She'd probably need her classmates to be gone in order to figure it out without being spotted and put in Mrs. Norrell's shoebox.

An empty classroom meant . . . lunch.

Lunch was at least an hour away.

Maybe Madison could use the time in between now and then to come up with an activism project idea that was good enough to win the vote. Yes! She knew just where to look for inspiration.

She jumped off her schoolbag and darted back into the dusty area beneath the bookshelves. She passed under a delicate spider's web as she raced toward the door that led from the classroom into the hallway. It was shut, but there was a gap underneath. It wasn't a very big gap . . . but Madison wasn't a very big mouse.

She used her whiskers to measure the opening. She stuck her head under the door. Then, she wriggled the rest of her body through the gap.

From her mouse point of view, the hallway was *enormous*. The fact that her vision was blurry and her eyes couldn't adjust to the bright lights only made everything seem larger and stranger. Luckily, she didn't have to see clearly to know which way to go. She was headed for one of her favorite places in the whole school.

She ran along the wall until she reached another door. She squirmed her way under that gap and paused with her pulse pounding hummingbird-fast in her chest. She looked up, up, up.

Stairs.

Her destination was on the second floor.

She thought she could climb the steps one at a time, digging her claws into the grippy rubber treads. But how long would that take? Madison looked over at the decorative metal curlicues that connected each stair to the wooden handrail. Could she get up to the railing? It seemed like it would be a lot faster—

Terrible idea, Great-Aunt Joelle grumbled in her mind. *You'd fall. Break your ankle—or all four ankles.*

Madison shuddered. Maybe her great-aunt was right. Maybe she should stay close to the ground. After all, she was pretty new to being a mouse.

She tackled the first stair, jumping to grab the edge of the step with her front paws and then pulling herself up onto the flat part. That wasn't so bad. She did it again. And again. And again. And again. And again.

Her body was getting tired, but she didn't have time to stop and rest.

Why were there so many stairs in this school, anyway?

She pushed herself to keep going. When she finally got to the second floor, she felt like she was at the top of Mount Everest. It had been an epic climb.

Muscles still twitching from the hard work, she flattened herself to pass under yet another closed door. She ran to the end of this hallway and stopped in front of a set of double doors. These were swung widely, invitingly open.

It was the library.

Madison loved the library. In here, she'd learned about kids (and grown-ups) who'd made a difference in the world. In here, she'd been inspired.

This Voice in Her Head

Madison ran to the nonfiction section, where the biographies were shelved. A biography is a story of a person's life. Mrs. Norrell had recently checked out a book from this section about kids who were doing big things. She'd been reading the class one chapter a day as part of their activism unit.

Thanks to that book, Madison knew about Marley Dias's #1000BlackGirlBooks drive and Mari Copeny's efforts to get safe water to her community. But Marley and Mari were only two of the amazing kids who were profiled. There were kids who tried to protect endangered animals. Kids who made sure every child in their town had school supplies. Kids who raised money for military veterans and kids who wanted to improve accessibility for disabled people and kids who gave speeches in front of their city council when they thought laws were unfair. These kids were leadership material.

If Madison won the class vote today, maybe one day there'd be a book about *her*.

She just needed the perfect idea.

There was no one in this part of the library, so Madison climbed up to the nonfiction shelf. As she scampered past the rows of books, she thought about how their school librarian, Ms. Washington, liked to say that the right book knew how to find the right person at the right time. Madison might not be a person at the moment, but maybe the right book would still find her.

She stopped in front of a story about a famous botanist, George Washington Carver.

A botanist is someone who studies plants. What if she proposed creating a community garden? Or a garden at their school? They could grow fruits and vegetables and herbs and—

You don't know anything about gardening, Great-Aunt Joelle interrupted.

Madison sighed and moved on to a book about a ballerina her mama liked, Misty Copeland. Maybe Madison could propose a project about the arts. Something like . . .

hosting free dance classes at the rec center downtown!

You don't know how to dance, Great-Aunt Joelle scoffed. *You've got two left feet. Literally, now that you're a mouse.*

Madison groaned. How was she supposed to think with this voice in her head?

She decided to take a closer look at the botanist's story. She climbed up and over the book, positioning herself against the shelf wall. She pushed against the edge of the cover. The book didn't budge. She pushed harder. The book was wedged in tight.

Madison tried to push out the next book in the row, and the next, and the next. None of them even wiggled. But she kept trying. She suddenly didn't care which book she knocked loose, as long as she moved something.

You're too small, her great-aunt said as Madison pushed and pushed.

"I am *not* too small!" Madison insisted. "I can do big things!"

You can't. You never will.

"I can! I can! I—" Madison pushed so hard, she lost her footing and fell down. As she lay on her back, breathing hard, she finally admitted defeat. "I can't."

Told you so, her great-aunt said smugly.

Madison had never had trouble believing in herself . . . until today. Today, she'd flunked every test. She hadn't been able to come up with a winning project idea. She hadn't been able to leap onto her chair to transform back into a human. She couldn't even push one library book off the shelf. Great-Aunt Joelle was right: she needed to be realistic about what she could and couldn't do.

Madison sighed. "I give up."

"Who are you talking to?" a voice asked.

"Nobody!" Madison squeaked, jumping to her four paws. "Who's there?"

"Over here!"

Madison saw a face—another mouse— peering around the corner of the divider that separated the nonfiction section from the picture books.

"Hello," the mouse said. "What brings you to my library?"

Peanut Butter Days

"Are you looking for something in particu-
lar?" the mouse asked. "Or just browsing?"

Madison said, "Um."

"I see that you're in the biography section.
The *C*s, to be precise."

"Um," Madison said again.

"Cat got your tongue?" The mouse giggled.
"Terrible joke. My apologies. Don't be fright-
ened. There are no cats here! Though this
would be the shelf for them. *Cat* starts with *c*,
you know."

"Um . . ."

"Actually, books about cats wouldn't be shelved here," the mouse said. "Biographies are about people, not animals."

Madison found her voice. "Can you . . . read?"

"A bit," the mouse said modestly.

"But . . . the books are so big. How do you move them?"

"Oh, I let the humans take care of that. I know my strengths, and . . ." The mouse laughed. "*Strength* isn't one of them."

"Okay, but . . . how did you learn to read?"

"This is a school," the mouse said, as if that explained everything. She crawled closer. "I'm Helene. What's your name?"

"Madison."

"Nice to meet you, Madison."

"Nice to meet you, too. Does Ms. Washington know you're here?"

"Of course not! Humans don't like to see mice running around. Best to stay out of sight."

Madison thought about the chaos in Mrs. Norrell's room right after she transformed. "I've learned that today," she said.

"Just today?" Helene asked curiously.

"It's my first day being a mouse." Hopefully it would be Madison's *only* day being a mouse, but she didn't say that part. She didn't want to insult Helene. "I'm supposed to be a person," she went on. "I turned into a mouse this morning."

"You're one of Bagel's children!" Helene sat back on her haunches and clapped her front paws with delight. "I've heard stories, but I've never met one of you! Tell me everything."

Helene listened intently as Madison told her about the car ride to school. About her notebook, filled with crossed-out ideas. About her transformation and her failed attempt to change back. About the trek up to the second floor and the heavy books she couldn't budge and her great-aunt's voice, echoing in her ears every step of the way.

"And then," Madison finished, "I met you."

Helene nodded thoughtfully. "Are you hungry?"

That wasn't the reaction Madison had been expecting.

"I have some bread in my nest," Helene went on. "One of the kindergarteners likes to hide her sandwich crusts under the cushions during story time. Sometimes, the crusts still have a smear of peanut butter." She closed her eyes and sighed. "Peanut butter days are the best."

Madison liked bread. She liked peanut butter. Now that she thought about it, she *was* hungry, after climbing all those stairs and pushing and pushing at the books. "Peanut butter sounds good."

"Then it's settled." Helene clapped her paws again and took off. "This way."

Madison followed Helene to the back corner of the library. She trailed the other mouse between two filing cabinets, through a small hole in the baseboard, and into a tiny, cozy room. There was a pile of cotton fluff in one corner. "From one of the story time cushions," Helene said. There were scraps of pages torn from books and magazines scattered across the floor. "Reading practice," Helene explained. Right in the center of the space, there were two bread crusts. "Lunch!" Helene squeaked gleefully. She nudged one of the crusts toward Madison.

Madison dug in. The bread was soft. The peanut butter was the perfect mix of sweet and salty. She chewed, swallowed, and let out a contented sigh.

Helene nodded. "Peanut butter days."

The two of them munched in silence for several minutes.

When she was done, Helene wiped the crumbs from her furry face and paws and said, "You know, everyone has a Great-Aunt Joelle."

"They do?!" Madison exclaimed.

"Absolutely," Helene said. "Let me tell you about mine."

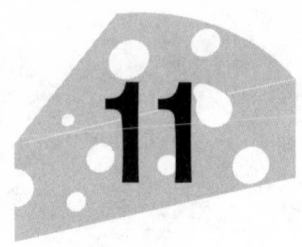

Be Quiet, Herbert

"**When I first came to the library,**" Helene began, "I didn't know what books were. But I started listening when Ms. Washington read aloud. Then I started looking at the books kids left out. When I discovered that the squiggly lines were *words* that came together to make *stories*, it was like a puzzle I had to solve. Figuring it all out would be more satisfying than the biggest, freshest peanut butter sandwich."

"Where does your Great-Aunt Joelle come in?" Madison asked.

"Oh, I don't have a Great-Aunt Joelle."

"But you said—"

"What I meant was, everyone has a voice in their head that tells them they can't do things. I call mine Herbert."

"Herbert?"

"Yes. When I decided to learn to read, Herbert said I was being silly. Mice don't read books! When I had trouble memorizing the alphabet, Herbert made sure to tell me I wasn't smart enough."

Madison frowned. "I don't think I like Herbert very much."

"Well, I don't like Great-Aunt Joelle." Helene paused. "The imaginary one. I'm sure the real one is lovely."

Madison bit her tongue. Her mama always said, if you couldn't say anything nice, you shouldn't say anything at all. And anyway, the exercise classes at the YMCA would definitely make the old woman more cheerful . . . someday.

"Do you know what I say to Herbert when he's talking too much?" Helene paused dramatically. "*Be quiet, Herbert.*"

Madison blinked. "That's it?"

"That's it."

"How does it work?"

"Herbert just says, 'No, no, no.' He doesn't give me any helpful advice. If he isn't going to be helpful"—Helene shrugged—"I don't need to listen to him."

"Wow," Madison said.

"I *knew* I could learn to read, if I worked at it," Helene added. "Listening to Herbert say 'No, no, no' was only slowing me down."

This morning, Madison had been so certain that she was leadership material. Then Great-Aunt Joelle had started talking . . . and Madison had listened.

"If you want to be a leader one day—"

"I want to be a leader *now*," Madison said. "But what if Great-Aunt Joelle is right?"

"Well, today probably isn't the only chance you'll ever get to show that you can be in charge," Helene said. "I didn't learn to read all in one day. It took time. And there are different ways of leading. What are your strengths?"

Madison and her dad had talked about this. "I'm organized. I like lists and plans."

"What else?"

"I'm good at making friends."

"Great! Keep going."

"I'm tidy. My mama likes that."

"I'm sure she does." Helene smiled.

Madison smiled back. But then the voice in her head said, *None of that means you'll be a leader.* Her smile dropped away.

"What happened just then?" Helene asked, leaning in.

"Great-Aunt Joelle." Madison looked at the floor. "She—"

"Tell her," Helene said firmly, "to be quiet."

"Be quiet, Great-Aunt Joelle," Madison muttered.

"With gusto!" Helene ordered.

"Be quiet, Great-Aunt Joelle!" Madison shouted, and then clapped a paw over her mouth.

"What's wrong?"

"Great-Aunt Joelle is a real person. She's an elder! I'm not supposed to talk back to my elders. It's disrespectful, and it's not good manners."

"Well, don't tell the *real* Great-Aunt Joelle to be quiet," Helene said. "Just the one in your mind."

"What if the *real* one is being negative, like in the car this morning?"

"Prove her wrong," Helene said fiercely.

Prove her wrong. Madison liked the sound of that.

"Okay," she said, "but 'Be quiet, Great-Aunt Joelle' still feels weird."

Helene tapped a claw against her sharp front teeth. "Could you use her initials?"

Madison tested it out. First, she pronounced each letter separately: *G, A, J.* Then, she tried saying it like the first half of the word *gadget*. That, she liked.

"Be quiet, GAJ," she said, and grinned.

Bell One

From deep inside Helene's cozy nest in the library wall, the ringing of the first lunch bell should have been muffled—but as a mouse, Madison heard it loud and clear. She swiveled her round ears on top of her head. "What time is it?"

Helene shrugged. "I can't tell time. I call it Bell One."

There were four midday bells. Mrs. Norrell's students went to the cafeteria at the first bell, and then back to their classroom for half an hour, and then to the playground or the gym for recess at the third bell.

Today, that half hour between lunch and recess was when Mrs. Norrell planned to hold the activism project vote. If Madison wanted to change back into a human being in time to get an idea on the ballot . . . she needed to get a move on.

You won't make it.

"Be quiet, GAJ," she muttered. To her astonishment, the old woman's voice faded away.

"Did it work?" Helene asked eagerly.

"Yes! This has been great," Madison said to Helene, moving toward the hole to exit the nest, "but I have to go."

"So soon?" Helene's whiskers drooped. "It's been nice having someone to talk to."

"I'll come back and find you, when I'm a person again," Madison said.

"That's sweet of you to say, but once you're a person, you won't understand me."

"What do you mean?"

"Humans don't speak Animal," Helene explained.

"Oh." Madison supposed that was why she'd never had a conversation with a mouse or a guinea pig—or any animal, for that matter—before today. "Well, I'll remember you. I'll bring you peanut butter sandwiches."

Helene gasped. "Really?"

"Really." Madison held up a paw to do a pinkie-promise, and then realized she couldn't hook pinkies with Helene. Their paws weren't built that way. All the more reason to change back into herself. There was nothing like a pinkie-promise to show you meant business. "I'm sorry. I have to hurry."

"Good luck with everything!" Helene called as Madison darted out into the library.

"Thank you!" Madison hollered back over her shoulder.

Madison ran through the open double doors and down the hall. She squeezed under the door that led to the stairwell. She skidded to a stop at the top of the stairs and looked over at the swirly metal banisters.

GAJ had said she'd fall if she tried to walk on the handrail.

But Madison didn't think she would.

She used her sharp nails to grab on to the lowest metal curlicue and pulled herself up. She stretched her body to clutch the next swirl. She went from one to the next until she reached the handrail. She swung up onto the wood surface. She made her way along the narrow railing. She quickly discovered that she could use her tail to help her balance, swinging it from side to side to match her gait.

Down, down, down.

By the time she reached the ground floor, she felt like she could fly.

Then she crawled under the door into the hallway and almost got stomped on by her own classmates, who were on their way to lunch.

"I brought ham and cheese," Riley said as Madison dodged her sparkly blue sneakers.

"I get cafeteria food today," Becca bragged. She was wearing shiny black dress shoes with thick rubber soles.

Madison pressed her body into the wall, wishing her fur blended in better with the tile. Her heart was doing the way-too-fast thing again. It felt like a lightning bolt was zigzagging around inside her.

Aaron and Zeke were the last kids in line. As they walked by her, Aaron ripped open his lunchbox. A snack flew out. It soared through the air, spinning and flipping, and landed a few inches from Madison's trembling whiskers.

"My Rice Krispies Treat!" Aaron crouched and grabbed the ziplock baggie. "That was a close one—" His eyes widened. "Zeke! Look!"

"Mrs. Norrell!" Zeke shouted. "We found the mouse!"

A Problem She Could Solve

Madison squeaked and ran. Her classmates chased her. Madison zipped around a corner and into a small crack in the baseboard. Outside in the hallway, she heard everyone slowing down.

"It was right there!" Aaron said.

"I'll let Mr. Bruce know." Mrs. Norrell sounded out of breath. "Let's go to lunch. And no more running in the halls!"

The footsteps moved in the opposite direction.

Madison emerged from the crack in the wall. She scurried toward Mrs. Norrell's room.

As she passed Mrs. Hoang's first-grade class-room, her sensitive ears picked up something that made her pause.

Someone was . . . calling for help? It was hard to tell, because the voice was a low hiss.

Madison wavered. She needed to return to her own classroom to transform back into herself. But she couldn't ignore a cry for help!

She decided to check it out. She squeezed under the door. Mrs. Hoang's first-graders went to recess at Bell One and lunch at Bell Two, so the room was empty.

"Help!"

The plea seemed to be coming from Mrs. Hoang's bearded dragon, Sprinkles. Madison ran toward the lizard's glass tank, which sat on a table near the teacher's desk.

"Hello?" she squeaked. "Sprinkles?"

A scratchy voice floated down. "Who's asking?"

"It's Madison Morris. I was in Mrs. Hoang's class last year. I gave you crickets."

Madison had been one of the first kids to volunteer to feed Sprinkles. Some of her classmates had been nervous to handle the container of live bugs. Madison had felt a little squeamish herself, but . . . bearded dragons ate crickets. She hadn't wanted Sprinkles to go hungry, so she'd raised her hand.

"What's wrong?" she asked now.

"You weren't in Mrs. Hoang's class," the lizard said, instead of answering the question.

"Was too!"

"Mrs. Hoang's students are all kids," Sprinkles argued. "Humans don't speak Animal. You and I are talking. Which means . . ." The bearded dragon approached his tank's glass wall and peered down at Madison. "See? You're not a kid. You're a mouse."

"I *am* a kid. I'm in Mrs. Norrell's class now. There's this thing that happens—"

"Oh. You're one of *those* kids," Sprinkles said. "Guess I'm not the only one with problems today."

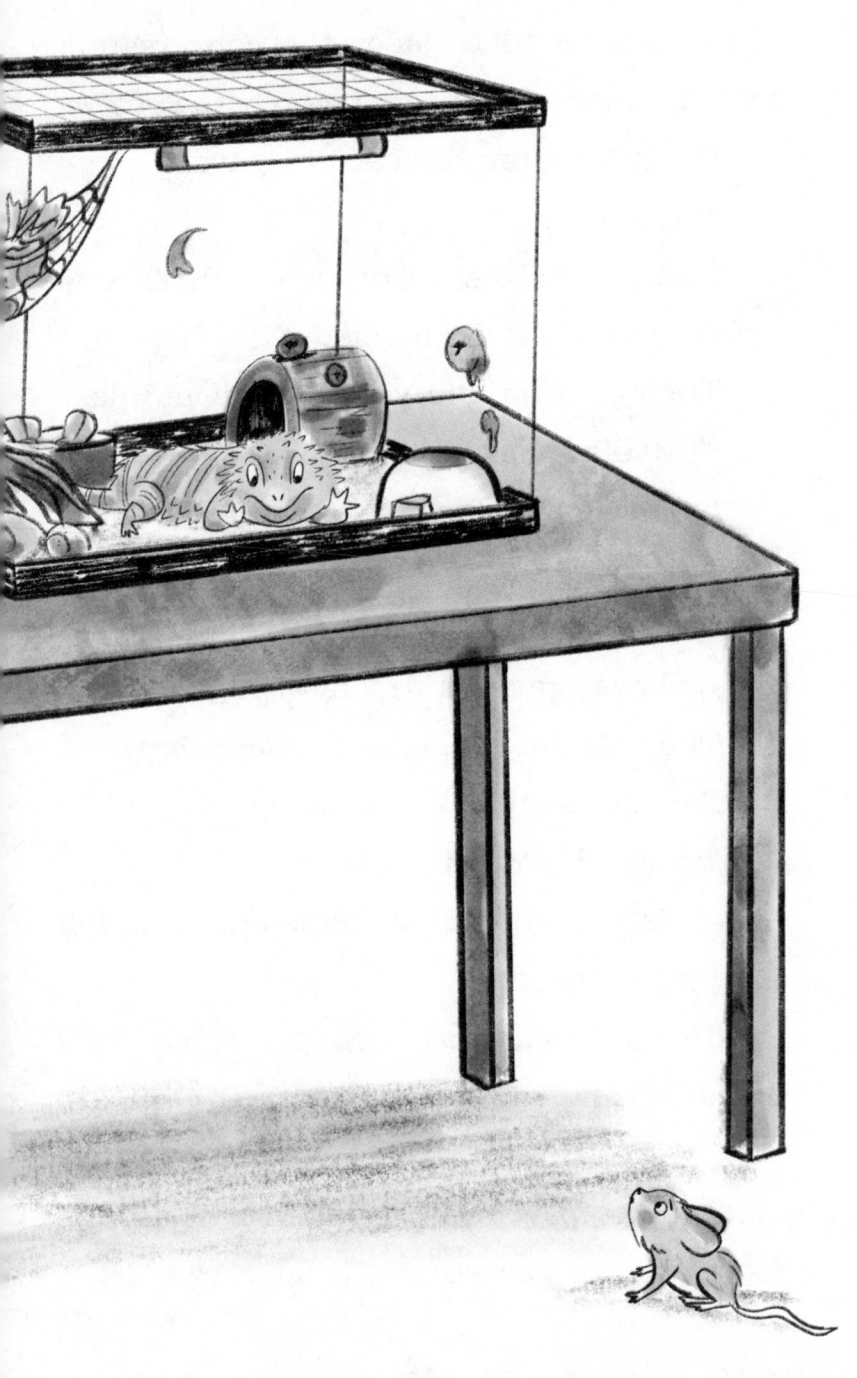

Madison tried to steer the conversation back on track. "What's going on with you?"

"Doesn't matter. You can't help me."

"Maybe I can."

"I don't need help from a kid. Even one who's not a kid at the moment."

"Then . . . who did you think would hear you?" Madison asked.

"I was hoping for one of the other class pets."

Madison sighed. "Well, you got *me*. What do you have against kids, anyway?"

"They're messy," the lizard said primly.

"*I'm* not messy."

The lizard hissed in disbelief.

Madison gathered her patience. "Just tell me what's wrong."

After a beat, Sprinkles grumbled, "It's embarrassing."

"I won't laugh. I swear." Madison put her right front paw over her heart. That was almost as good as a pinkie-promise.

Sprinkles muttered something.

"What did you say?" Madison asked.

"I said . . . I knocked over my fruit bowl. Again."

In addition to his daily crickets, Madison remembered the bearded dragon nibbling on pieces of fruit and lettuce. The food was usually tossed all around his habitat. "I thought you spread out your snacks on purpose," she said.

"I don't," the lizard snapped. "And there's nothing you can do about it, so you might as well leave me alone." He moved away from the glass, ending the conversation.

But beneath his tank, Madison realized something: This was a problem she could solve.

Like she'd told Sprinkles, Madison wasn't messy. Her strengths included being organized and tidy. And today, she was a mouse. That meant she could understand the lizard, which she could never have done as a human being.

"I can help!" she squeaked.

Sprinkles ignored her.

"I can!" she cried.

You can't, GAJ snarled inside her head.

"Be quiet, GAJ," Madison said, and she started coming up with a plan.

On Top of the World

Getting into the tank was going to be tricky.
The table it sat on had smooth, straight legs.
The tank itself was made of slick glass. It had
a mesh top, for airflow—that part, Madison
knew she could handle. Her sharp teeth and
claws could rip through the mesh in no time.
But how would she get up there?

Madison turned in a circle. She needed
something that was tall, sturdy, and rough
enough for her to climb up to the tank roof,
but that was also lightweight enough for her
to push or pull as a mouse. She didn't see anything.

"You're wasting your time," Sprinkles grumbled.

"I'm not." In fact, Madison was feeling more determined by the second. She looked at Mrs. Hoang's desk, and then at the teacher's rolling chair. The chair looked like it had a lot of textured surfaces to grip . . .

She climbed up one of the wheels. She ran along the leg. She spiraled around the base leading to the back of the chair. She dug her claws into the soft cushion and pulled herself onto the seat. She jumped to one plastic arm and dashed straight across to where it bumped into the wooden desk. She crossed the desk, climbed onto a stack of books near the edge, and looked into Sprinkles's cage.

The lizard's fruit bowl was upside-down. There was food *everywhere*.

Apple chunks in the water bowl. Blueberries on the basking log. Watermelon cubes strewn across the ground. Small pieces of lettuce scattered about like crisp green confetti.

In the middle of it all sat the grouchy, spiky lizard.

Sprinkles gave Madison a resentful look. "It's a disaster," he said.

"It's not so bad," she assured him.

"Either way, there's nothing you can do—"

"I'm going to fix it."

How can you possibly help? GAJ asked. *You're just a mouse.*

"Be quiet, GAJ," Madison murmured.

She looked at the distance from the desk to the glass tank. Was it jumpable?

It was far—much farther than the leap from her backpack to her chair had been this morning, and she hadn't been able to make that. But . . . here, she could get a running start across the length of Mrs. Hoang's desk. Also, she'd now been a mouse for hours. She knew how to use her tail for balance. How to let her whiskers sense which way the air was moving.

Maybe, just maybe . . . she could make it.

"I wouldn't do that if I were you," Sprinkles said grimly.

He's right, GAJ chimed in. *Don't even try.*

"I can make it," Madison said, ready to prove them wrong.

She darted to the opposite end of the teacher's desk. She crouched, gathering power in her back legs. She pushed off. She ran fast—faster—faster than she'd ever run before. She raced up the small stack of books and, without slowing down even a little bit, catapulted herself into the air.

She soared. The mesh tank lid got closer and closer. Madison stretched her tiny body. She reached . . . and reached . . .

Her claws brushed the edge of the lid. One nail managed to hook into the mesh.

One nail was all it took. Madison bounced off the glass tank wall and swung her other paw up to the rim. She pulled herself up to sit on the mesh, heart pounding triple-time.

She felt like she was on top of the world.

Nothing But Possibilities

"I . . . didn't think you could jump that far," Sprinkles said, staring up at her.

"Well, I made it," Madison replied, "so let's fix your fruit bowl!" She dashed around the rim of the tank lid, past the mounted heat lamp, and stopped when she spotted a loose piece of mesh. She bit it, tugging and gnawing to create a hole in the roof. "Can you move your basking log?" she asked.

Sprinkles trudged over to the end of the log and nudged it with his nose until the tallest point was underneath Madison. "I don't know why you're bothering. This is pointless."

Madison slipped through the hole in the mesh, dropped down to the log, and darted along it to stand beside Sprinkles. "Helping is never pointless," she said.

The bearded dragon rolled his eyes.

Madison examined the habitat. The ground looked like sand but was actually more like a bumpy rubber carpet. So, there'd be no digging a hole to put the fruit bowl in . . . but maybe the sticky surface would be helpful. The basking log was made out of real wood, smooth and splinter-free with a variety of interesting knobs and branches. Madison ran under and over and around it, examining it from all angles and seeing nothing but possibilities.

Sprinkles watched her with narrowed eyes. "What are you doing?"

"This gap," Madison said, wriggling through an opening between the log and the floor. "Do you think we could wedge your fruit bowl in here, so it doesn't flip as easily?"

The bearded dragon sighed. "I don't know. Probably not."

"Let's try." Madison ran to the empty container. She grabbed the rim with her teeth and dragged it over to the log. She stuck its edge into the gap, let go of her mouth-grip, and used the side of her furry body to push it in farther. She pushed and pushed until she felt like the bowl was good and stuck.

She stepped back to look at her handiwork.

"It's crooked," Sprinkles said critically.

"A little," Madison admitted. "Does that bother you?"

"Yes," the lizard said.

"As much as having your fruit scattered everywhere?"

There was a very, *very* long pause before Sprinkles begrudgingly said, "No."

"Great!" Madison zipped around, collecting apple chunks and blueberries and watermelon cubes and lettuce confetti. In minutes, the tank was practically spotless. "Ta-da!"

Sprinkles turned in a circle, grunting to himself. He huffed air in and out of his nostrils.

Madison almost couldn't stand the suspense.

Then the lizard faced her, and his mouth opened in a wide smile.

That smile made Madison feel so proud. That smile . . . it was better than homemade cherry cobbler and llamas and sunflowers combined.

"You did it," Sprinkles said. "Thank you."

"Happy to help," Madison answered—and she really, really was.

But then, out in the hallway, Bell Two chimed.

Mrs. Norrell's class was about to return from lunch! Madison was running out of time! She darted up onto the basking log and was all set to jump to the lid—

"Wait!" Sprinkles said, his smile fading away. "What if Mrs. Hoang moves the fruit bowl when she feeds me or cleans my tank?"

"Put it back in the same spot. If you do that a few times, she should figure out that that's where you want it." It was like how Mrs. Norrell knew that Madison usually raised her hand to be called on first, and so today, she'd called on Madison first, even *without* a hand-raise. But just in case . . . "I'll check on you, when I'm a person," Madison promised. "If the bowl's in the wrong place, I can move it."

"Hm," the bearded dragon said. "That sounds . . . fine."

Madison jumped up to catch her claws in the mesh ceiling. She made her way down to the floor. "Bye, Sprinkles!" she yelled, before squeezing herself under the closed door.

A Better Idea

Madison dashed down the hall, whiskers brushing the wall. She turned the corner, heading toward Mrs. Norrell's room, and saw her classmates filing inside. Mrs. Norrell stood at the entrance, counting heads. Madison stopped to watch.

She'd been a mouse for hours. Even if she had gone to the office to call her parents, like Tally had said, she'd be back by now. Why didn't Mrs. Norrell seem to care? Was this what Bagel had meant when he'd said everyone else was a little . . . foggy?

No one's foggy, GAJ snapped. *Your teacher just doesn't care about you.*

"Be quiet, GAJ."

You took too long helping that lizard, GAJ taunted. *You missed the empty classroom time. Now you'll have to wait until recess to change back. You'll be a mouse during the project vote, and no one will ever hear your ideas—not that they were any good, anyway—*

"Be quiet!" Madison squealed, putting her front paws on either side of her head.

It was like what Helene had said about Herbert: GAJ wasn't helpful. GAJ wanted Madison to focus on everything she couldn't do. But Madison didn't like thinking that way. Thinking that way definitely didn't make Madison feel like leadership material.

Stopping to help Sprinkles fix his fruit bowl hadn't been a mistake.

And what if missing the empty classroom time wasn't as bad as GAJ made it out to be? What if Madison didn't need to jump and jump and jump to make it onto her chair? What if she was strong enough now to get up there on the first try?

She didn't wait to hear what GAJ had to say about that.

After Mrs. Norrell ushered her last student into the classroom, Madison darted forward. She squeezed under the door. Inside the classroom, she stayed out of sight beneath the bookshelves as she raced toward her desk in the second row.

She ran fast—faster—faster than she would have thought possible—and as she ran, she thought about making that giant leap from Mrs. Hoang's desk to Sprinkles's tank. She zipped out from under the shelves. She dashed up her backpack. She flung herself into the air, aiming for her seat . . .

She made it!

She hit the slick surface and slid sideways.

Oh, no. She couldn't stop. She scratched with her claws, trying to slow down. What would happen if she fell right off the other side of the chair?

You'll be a mouse forever.

"No!" she squeaked. "I will not! Be quiet, GAJ!"

She smelled a strange, skunky, citrus air-freshener smell.

There was a distant pop, like someone had stuck a pin into a balloon.

A cool breeze ruffled her fur . . . which suddenly wasn't fur at all.

It was warm brown skin.

Madison was sitting at her desk, and she was herself again. She ran her hands over her corn-rows—which she loved, no matter what Great-Aunt Joelle or anyone else thought. She smiled, and then she wrinkled her nose and twitched her lips from side to side like she was wiggling her whiskers.

But she no longer had whiskers.

Thank goodness.

Her classmates were blinking and shaking their heads. Lydia was the first to recover.

"Madison!" she squealed. "Mrs. Norrell! Madison's here!"

The teacher cleared her throat. "Madison," she said. "Welcome back."

"Thanks." Madison stood. "Is it okay if I do my presentation now?"

"Of course," Mrs. Norrell said. "We're all excited to hear what you have to say."

Madison looked down at her brainstorming notebook. She decided to leave it where it was. After everything that had happened to her today . . . she had a better idea.

Her Usual Amazing Self

Madison went to stand by the chalkboard. "I actually came up with a lot of ideas," she began. "But all of your ideas this morning were really great. I think we should vote on those." She looked at Mrs. Norrell. "I want to propose something a little different, if that's okay."

"Go ahead," the teacher said.

"It's important for us to do things to help our community now," Madison said. "But not *just* now. This can be . . . the beginning."

The beginning was a fine place to be. Helene had taught Madison that.

"I want to be a leader one day," Madison told her classmates. "And I bet some of you do, too. My idea is, what if we bring in community leaders to talk to us about how they got where they are? What keeps them going when things don't work out the way they wanted—when they feel like they failed? Hearing from them will give all of us"—how would her dad put it?—"tools," she finished. "For our leadership toolbox."

That sounded right. It seemed like something a boss would say.

For once, GAJ didn't offer any arguments.

"That," Mrs. Norrell said, "is a wonderful idea."

Madison flushed with pride. "I could put together a list of people we could reach out to."

"Excellent. Thank you." Mrs. Norrell gestured for Madison to return to her seat. Then she picked up a stack of papers. "Okay, time to vote! Remember, you can rank your three favorite project ideas." She began handing out the ballots.

Lydia leaned over to whisper to Madison. "That was awesome. Good job!"

"You too," Madison said. She hadn't had the chance to tell her best friend that earlier. She'd been too busy panicking and turning into a mouse. Speaking of which . . . "Lydia," she said, "you won't believe what happened to me—"

"Madison!" Tally yelped from two rows back. "Can I talk to you for a second?"

"Tally, is everything all right?" Mrs. Norrell asked.

"Yes," Tally said. "I just need to tell Madison something."

"All right," Mrs. Norrell said, "but make it quick."

Madison went to Tally's desk. Tally motioned for her to lean in close, and then murmured, "Were you about to tell Lydia about transforming into a mouse?"

Madison gaped at her. "How did you know?"

"How did I know what you were going to tell Lydia, or that you were the mouse?"

"Um . . . both?"

"Do you remember the turtle on the first day of school?"

Madison nodded.

Tally giggled. "That was me! Anyway, didn't Bagel explain? The animal thing has to stay a secret—"

"Okay, girls," Mrs. Norrell said, placing a ballot between them on Tally's desk. "You can finish this at recess. Back to your seat, Madison."

"We'll talk more later," Tally said, eyes gleaming with excitement.

"You bet we will!" Madison returned to her chair.

"What was that about?" Lydia asked.

"Nothing."

"What were you going to tell me?"

Madison looked over her shoulder at Tally. Then she said, "It was Great-Aunt Joelle."

Lydia made a face. "What'd she do?"

"In the car this morning on the way to school, she was really negative. She messed with my head. I've been hearing her voice all day, telling me I can't do stuff."

"Oh," Lydia said, nodding with understanding. She'd met Madison's great-aunt. "Well, I would never have known. You seem like your usual amazing self to me."

Madison grinned. She *felt* like her usual amazing self.

And that was . . . well, it was *amazing*.

Ten Fun Facts about House Mice

 1 The term *house mouse* refers to one of the most populous species in the mouse family. House mice can be found in nearly every country on the planet. While they've been domesticated as pets and laboratory animals, even the wild ones are known for living in and around human dwellings—hence their name.

2 The average house mouse is three to four inches long, with a two- to four-inch-long tail. Mice grow fast, so as a juvenile, Madison is already almost full-size. In the wild, they tend to have gray, brown, or black fur. Domesticated mice can be bred to have white, spotted, or shiny "satin" coats. (These are also known as "fancy" mice!)

3 According to the Guinness Book of World Records, the longest-lived pet mouse was Fritzy, who lived seven years and seven months (he died in 1985). The average life span of a domesticated mouse is two to three years. In the wild, where they face many predators, mice may live less than a year.

4 Mice don't have great eyesight. Their eyes are sensitive to bright light, and they don't see well in the dark. Their other senses make up the difference. They have excellent hearing, keen noses, and a secret weapon: whiskers. Mice use their whiskers to gather information about the world around them. They brush their whiskers across surfaces to identify and map them. Whiskers can also detect vibrations from airflow, sound waves, and nearby predator movement.

Madison's mouse-voice comes out as a high squeak. When mice interact with each other, they may squeak, chirp, or even "sing." Mice will alter their pitch and volume depending on what they're trying to communicate—for instance, if they've found food or sense danger. Some mouse noises are so high-pitched that humans can't hear them at all.

 It's no wonder Madison feels like her heart is racing after she transforms: a mouse's heart beats almost twelve times a second! By comparison, a human's resting heart rate is about one beat per second.

 Why do mice love to gnaw on things? Because their front teeth literally never stop growing. To whittle down those incisors (and to get into places they don't belong), mice will chew through wood, plastic, aluminum, vinyl, electrical wiring, and many other materials.

Mice are outstanding climbers, able to scale rough surfaces using their toenails for grip. They have a vertical jump of approximately twelve inches and can run up to eight miles per hour. They're also strong swimmers and can walk along thin ropes and wires.

A mouse's biggest body part is its skull, so if its head fits through a gap, the body should be able to follow. A full-grown mouse can squeeze through a hole the size of a dime. If a mouse finds a hole that isn't quite large enough . . . that's where those sharp teeth come in handy.

10 Fancy mice make great pets, as they're friendly, intelligent, active, and don't take up much space. Because rodents can carry diseases, you should always wash your hands after you handle a pet mouse or clean its habitat. Also, avoid kissing or nuzzling these animals. And remember: if you hear or see a mouse you *didn't* buy at the pet store, tell an adult.

Acknowledgments

Thanks to:

- My editor, Erica Finkel, for helping me get to the heart of the story.

- My agent, Alyssa Eisner Henkin, for constantly pushing me forward.

- Ariel Landy and Okan Bülbül, for their beautiful artwork; and Jade Rector, Deena Fleming, and Brann Garvey for their design expertise.

- The rest of the Amulet team—Emily Daluga, Megan Carlson, Jenn Jimenez, Maggie Lehrman, and Andrew Smith—for shepherding this series to publication, as well as publicist Mary Marolla, for working so hard to spread the word about Class Critters.

- Janae Marks, for her thoughtful notes on the completed manuscript, and Abbi Crutchfield, for generously answering first-draft questions.

- My friends and family, for encouraging me to do big things—and for cheering when they happen.
- Justin, for always standing beside me, and Evie, for being her usual amazing self.

About the Author

Kathryn Holmes always dreamed of telling stories for a living. These days, she writes books for kids and teens. Originally from Maryville, Tennessee, she went to Goucher College in Baltimore, Maryland, where she majored in dance and English literature. She later received her MFA in writing for children from the New School in New York City. Kathryn now lives in Brooklyn, New York, with her husband and daughter. You can find her online at kathrynholmes.com.